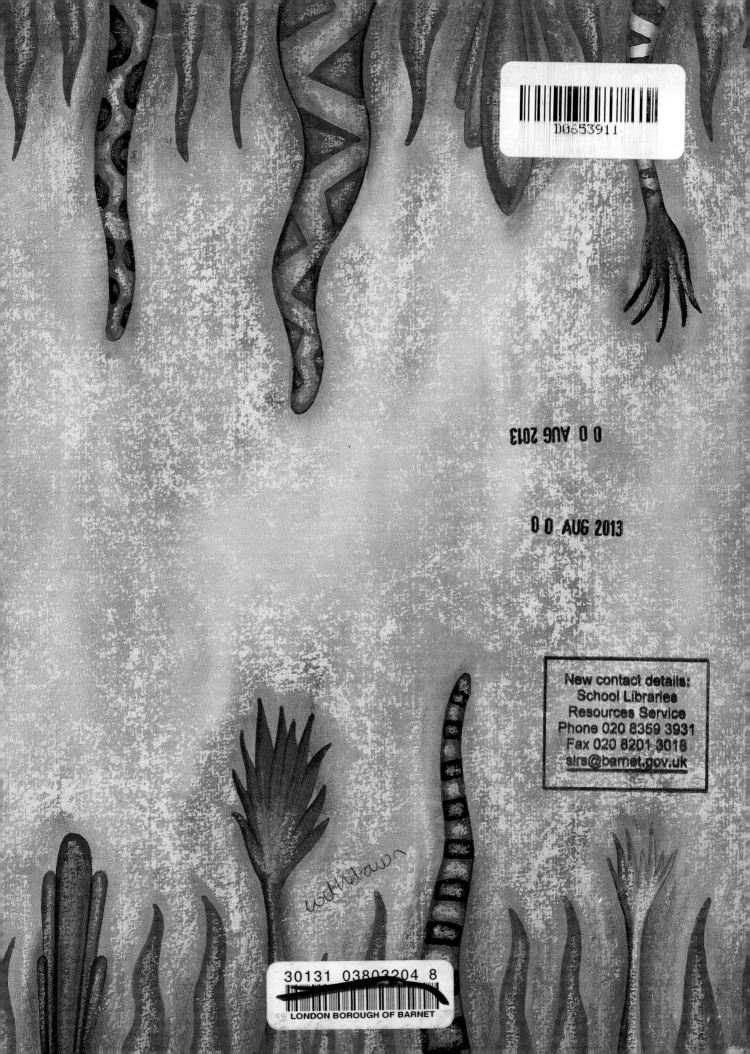

To Oliver, Emily and
Henry with love

First published in the United Kingdom in 2002 by Ragged Bears Publishing Limited,
Milborne Wick, Sherborne, Dorset DT9 4PW

Distributed by Ragged Bears Limited, Ragged Appleshaw, Andover, Hampshire SP11 9HX
Tel: 01264 772269

A CIP record of this book is available from the British Library

ISBN 1 85714 253 5

Printed in China

The Clever Rat
and other
African Tales

BASED ON OLD EAST AFRICAN STORIES,

RETOLD BY
Suzi Lewis-Barned

ILLUSTRATED BY
Karen Perrins

Milborne Wick, Dorset • Brooklyn, New York

African Tales

Introduction/Acknowledgements

My father, John Lewis-Barned, first came across these stories when he was learning Swahili in 1950, in preparation for working in East Africa. When he returned to England in the 1960s he was asked to teach Swahili to students in Oxford. He asked various friends for Swahili books and was lucky enough to be sent a copy of the original collection from which these have been selected and re-told. The 1946 edition states that they are 'Swahili stories told and written down by Africans put into standard orthography by a Reader of the Inter-territorial Language Committee of East Africa', a team of seventeen members convened by the three countries of East Africa (Kenya, Uganda and Tanganyika) in 1930. As far as we are aware, none of the stories has ever been translated into English before.

As their eight grandchildren grew up, my parents wanted them to know and love the stories as much as the children in East Africa do. (They have been re-printed at least forty-two times there). They passed the translations to me and asked me to re-tell them for our children. They were too good to keep just for ourselves and I hope other children will enjoy them as much as we have.

My thanks to my parents, John and Ursula, for the original translations, and for their help and advice. Also to Macmillan Education Ltd. for granting us the translation and publishing rights and to Barbara Turfan of the School of African and Oriental Studies for helping to trace the origin of the stories. Thanks also to my husband, David Jacobs, for his patience and support and to the rest of the family and our friends who shared the stories with their children and helped select ten of the best for this collection.

Suzi Lewis-Barned
July 2001

Contents

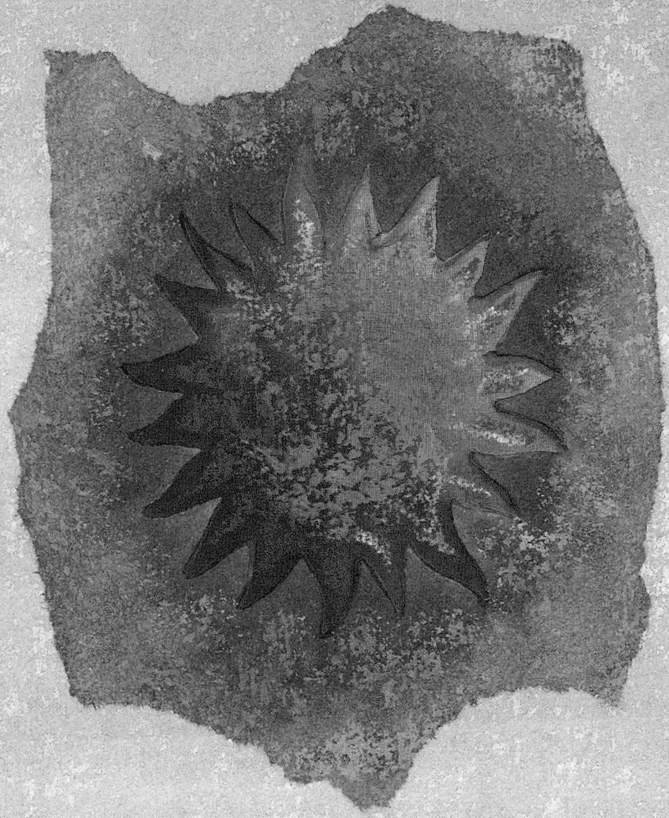

The Clever Rat

One day a farmer went into his grain store to discover that something had been eating through his bags of millet. "This is the work of a rat," said the farmer to his wife. "I shall set a trap to catch him and then I will kill him with my stick."

The rat, who was old and very clever, saw the trap and knew exactly what would happen to him if he were caught, but it had been placed between him and the millet so he would have to go hungry or risk capture. He decided to ask the farm animals to help him, so he went across the farmyard to see the cockerel.

"My friend Cock," said the rat, "be so good as to spring that trap so that I may have my supper." But the cockerel replied, "Me? Spring a trap for you? Phooey! It is no business of mine. Go away, Rat." And he kicked dust in Rat's face as he strutted off.

"Just remember," called Rat, shaking the dust off his sleek, glossy coat, "today it is my trap, but tomorrow it may be yours."

Then the clever rat went to see the goat who was tethered by some rough grass at the edge of the field. "My friend Goat," said Rat, "be so good as to spring that trap so I may have my supper." But the goat replied, "Me? Spring a trap for you? Phooey! It is no business of mine. Go away, Rat." And he butted Rat so hard that he flew up into the air and landed on the other side of the field.

"Just remember," called Rat, picking himself up and checking to see whether he had broken any bones (which he hadn't), "today it is my trap, but tomorrow it may be yours."

11

Then the clever rat went to the cow, who was chewing on the green grass in a beautiful field which sloped down to a running river. "My friend Cow," said Rat, "be so good as to spring that trap so I may have my supper." But the cow replied, "Me? Spring a trap for you? Phooey! It is no business of mine. Go away, Rat." And she dropped a large cowpat on top of Rat's head. "Just remember," said Rat, as he hurried to wash himself in the river, "today it is my trap, but tomorrow it may be yours."

Then the clever rat saw a snake slithering through the grass. Snakes kill rats so the rat scuttled away as fast as he could. He hurried back to the grain store, pursued by the snake, and managed to avoid the trap as he leapt up on top of a bag of millet. But the snake did not see the trap and it snapped shut on him, leaving him writhing furiously inside.

It was the middle of the night when the farmer heard the trap snap shut. He took a stick and hurried to the store. "Don't you think you ought to take a lamp with you?" asked his wife. "It's only that rat. I don't need one," he reassured her. But when he reached the store and struck the snake with his stick it bit him and he screamed out in pain, "Quick! Wife! I am dying!"

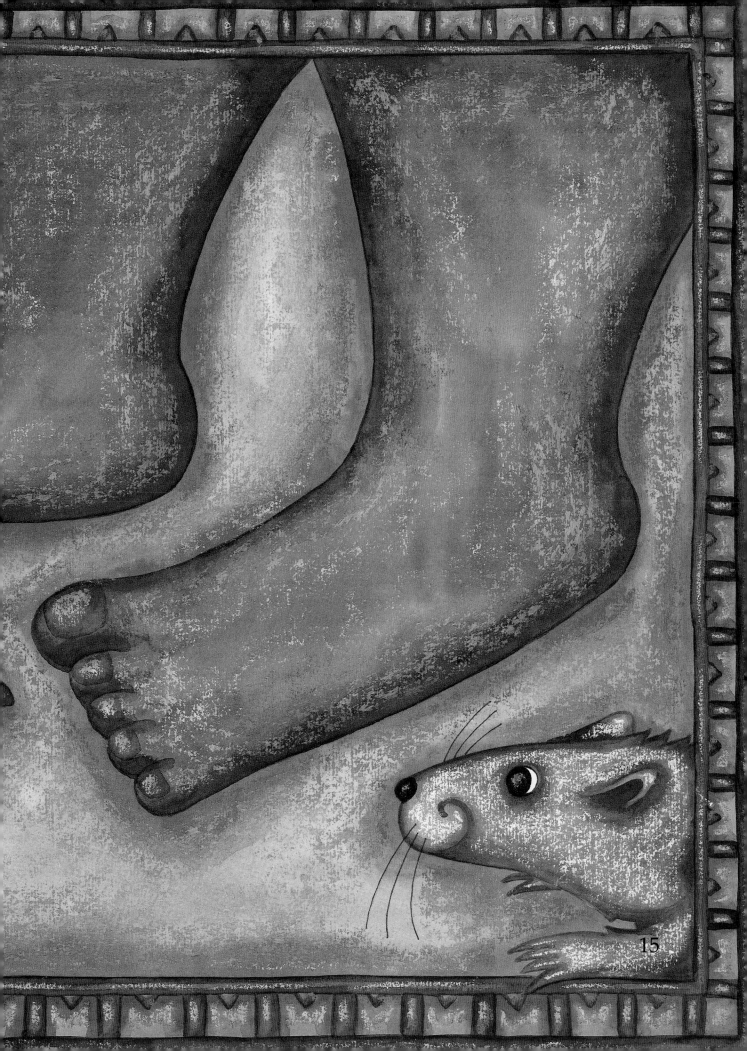

15

His wife rushed to the grain store with the lamp, and when she saw what had happened she shouted for help. But it was too late: the farmer was already dead. When morning came, the farmer's family came to his house to mourn their loss and that night they killed the cock for their meal.

The next day many more people came to comfort the farmer's wife, and she prepared a feast, for some had travelled a long way. She killed the goat for the meal they were to have. And on the day of the funeral, the cow was taken and killed for the wake which followed it.

And so the clever rat's prophecy came true. Although the trap had been set for him, he had escaped and the other animals had lost their lives because they had refused to help him. If only they had sprung the trap no one would have been caught, and their lives would all have been saved.

The clever rat lived for many more years in the farmyard
and farmers today still suffer from his descendants who
can almost always be found near the grain store.

The Wisest
Of Cats

Once upon a time there was a cat who lived
all alone. But he was rather a small cat and he
needed someone to look after him. One day
the cat said to himself, "It's not good for me to
be all alone. I need someone to look after me.
I'm going to look for a Big Strong Friend."

He hadn't gone very far when he met Zebra. "Will you be my Big Strong Friend and protect me from all harm?" he mewed up to Zebra in his tiny voice. "I am the strongest and bravest of all beasts," replied Zebra. "I will be your Big Strong Friend." So the cat stayed with Zebra and he felt very safe.

But one day when Zebra was grazing on the wide grasslands, he was chased by Lion. He managed to escape by galloping away to join his friends who were also being chased. The little cat was very surprised. "You said you were the strongest and bravest of all beasts, but you ran away from Lion so he must be stronger and braver than you," he said. "I'm going to ask him to be my Big Strong Friend." So the little cat ran up to Lion, and mewed up to him in his tiny voice, "Will you be my Big Strong Friend and protect me from all harm?"

"I am the strongest and bravest of all beasts," replied Lion. "I will be your Big Strong Friend." So the cat stayed with Lion and he felt very safe.

One day while the cat and the Lion were walking in the forest they were chased by Elephant. They only just managed to escape from him by climbing into the tall branches of a tree. The little cat was amazed. "I thought you were the strongest and bravest of all beasts but Elephant is stronger and braver than you," he said. "I'm going to ask him to be my Big Strong Friend."

21

So the little cat ran after Elephant and
mewed up to him in his tiny voice,
"Will you be my Big Strong Friend and
protect me from all harm?"

"I am the strongest and bravest of all
beasts," replied Elephant. "I will be
your Big Strong Friend."

A long time passed. Cat and Elephant
became the greatest of friends. Then
one day they were walking together in
the forest when they saw Man. Man
pointed his gun at Elephant and he ran
away as fast as he could. The cat was
amazed. "I thought you were the
strongest and fiercest of all the beasts,
but Man is stronger and fiercer than
you," he said. "I'm going to ask him
to be my Big Strong Friend."

So the little cat ran after Man and mewed up to him in his tiny voice, "Will you be my Big Strong Friend and protect me from all harm?"

"I am stronger and braver than all the beasts in the jungle," replied Man. "I will be your Big Strong Friend." Then he bent down and gently picked up the little cat and took him home. When they got there, the hunter's wife took the gun and ammunition from him at once and the cat was astonished that he did not say a word, but flopped down into the nearest chair.

"How easily Woman took Man's weapons from him," thought the cat in surprise. "Now I know who is really the strongest and bravest creature in the jungle," he said to himself, but he was careful to whisper so Man could not hear.

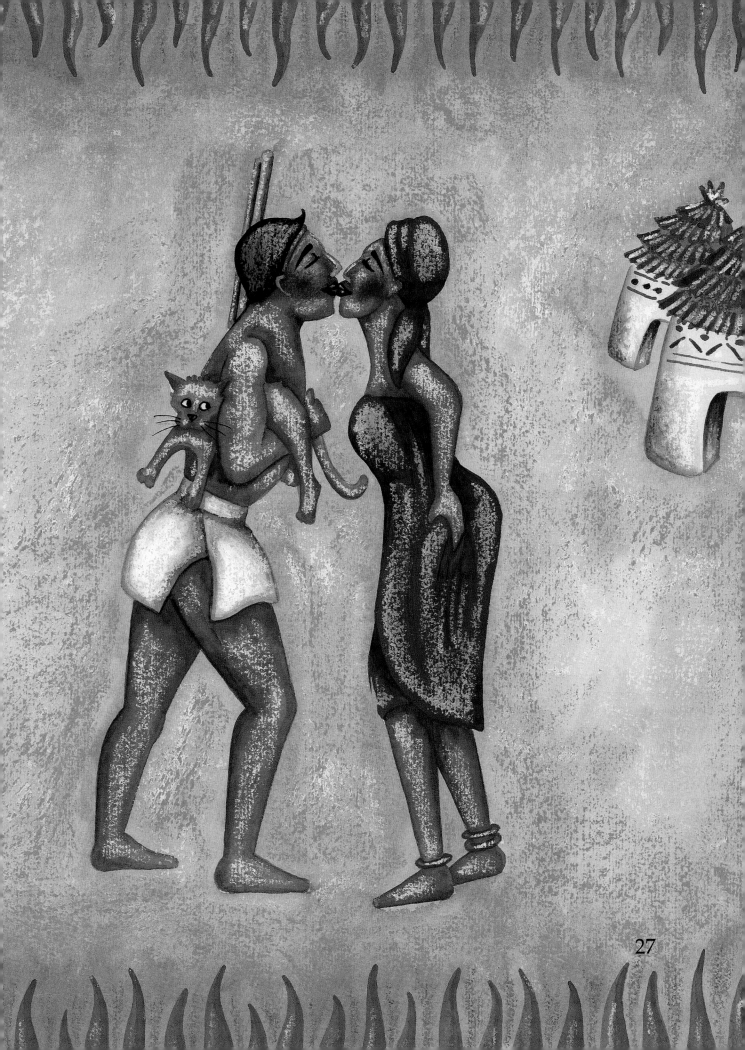

He crept into the kitchen where Woman was busy preparing Man's supper and rubbed gently against her legs. "Will you be my Big Strong Friend and protect me from all harm?" he asked her. "Yes, if you will guard my kitchen from rats and mice, and keep me company when Man goes hunting," replied Woman.

And that is why, even today, you will find that the wisest of cats stays close to the kitchen.

Fikirini
And Hemedi

Long ago in the land of Pate lived a Master Tailor
who owned a large shop with twenty apprentices.
Amongst them was one called Fikirini.

Fikirini was very good at his job, but he was
also very vain and he liked to imagine that he
was very grand. He made friends with the sons
of Sultans, not because he liked them, but because
they were powerful and important. He began to
dress like them, with much finery and silk, and
when people greeted him he acknowledged
them by touching his head with his hand, just
as Sultans do.

As time went by Fikirini became so convinced of his own importance that he began to believe he would make a better Sultan's son than any of his friends.

One day the Master Tailor asked Fikirini to mend a Sultan's robe. Fikirini worked late to finish it, and when all the other apprentices had gone home, he put it on, looked in the mirror and struck his most Sultanly pose. "This is indeed my lucky day," he said to himself. "Now I shall truly be the son of a Sultan."

That night Fikirini left the land of Pate to seek his fortune dressed in the Sultan's robe, and he looked so like a Sultan's son that everyone he met along the road bowed down before him. After he'd been travelling for a few days, Fikirini met a real Sultan's son, whose name was Hemedi.

"Hello," said Fikirini. "Where are you going?"

"I don't know," said Hemedi. "I am feeling very confused. What about you?"

"I'm not sure either," said Fikirini. So they tied up their horses, got out their food, and sat down for a long chat.

"Tell me your story," said Fikirini to Hemedi. "Well, until last week I thought I was the son of the Sultan of Guba," began Hemedi. "He brought me up as his son but a few days ago, on my twenty-first birthday, he told me that I'm really the son of the great Sultan of Baghdad." "How come?" asked Fikirini. "On the day I was born, some wise men came to see my father and told him that he should send me away because evil men were planning to kill me. They told him that I should not return to my father's kingdom for twenty-one years," explained Hemedi.
"But after all that time, how will your father know you are his son?" asked Fikirini. "When he left me with the Sultan of Guba he gave him this dagger for me to bring back so he will know I am truly his son," explained Hemedi.

Then Fikirini told Hemedi about his ambition to be rich and powerful. "I may only be an apprentice tailor, but I know I am destined for better things," he said. Hemedi promised to help him become the most rich and famous tailor in Baghdad when he became the Sultan.

But after Hemedi had gone to sleep that night, Fikirini stole his dagger and his horse and set off for Baghdad. He galloped up to the palace gates and shouted, "I am Hemedi, the son of the Sultan!" And the guards rushed to tell Hemedi's father, the old Sultan.

Fikirini took Hemedi's dagger from its sheath and handed it to the old man, who hugged him and said, "Praise be to God, who has brought my precious son home to me. Let there be a great feast in his honour, and much rejoicing." Then all the people shouted, "Hemedi has come home! Hemedi has come home! Praise be to God!"

34

The Sultan took Fikirini into the palace. "Come and see your mother," he said.

But Fikirini held back. "There's something I have to tell you first," he said. "While I was making my way home I met an impostor who claims to be your son, but he's really just a tailor's apprentice." "Indeed," replied the Sultan. Then he led the way to the palace, where his wife had already heard of her son's arrival. "Go on in and greet your mother," said the Sultan. But when she saw Fikirini, the Sultan's wife said, "This is not my son. I may not have seen him since he was a baby, but a mother knows her own son - and this is not he."

Just then Hemedi, who had woken to find Fikirini and his horse gone, and had followed behind him as quickly as he could, rushed into the palace, shouting, "Mother, it is I! Please believe me! This impostor is just a common tailor's apprentice!" The Sultan, who believed what Fikirini had told him, ordered Hemedi to be thrown in the dungeons. But when the Sultan's wife saw Hemedi, she was convinced that he was indeed her son. "I have a plan which will prove to you which of the two men is our son," she said to her husband.

The next morning the two young men were summoned before the Sultan and Sultana. They were each ordered to make a cloak, fit for the Sultan himself.

Fikirini knew that to make the cloak would be easy for him. "I shall make a cloak that will fill everyone with wonder," he said. But Hemedi was lost for words, because he'd never even sewn on a button before. Fikirini made a really beautiful cloak, but Hemedi didn't even cut out the cloth.

"Why have you not done as I ordered?" roared the Sultan. "I don't know how to cut cloth, because Sultans' sons have tailors to sew for them," replied Hemedi.

Now the Sultana was convinced he was her son, but the Sultan decided to put the pair to a final test, just to be certain. He had two boxes made. On the top of the first box, which was encrusted with pearls, was inscribed: 'I Seek Wealth And Fortune' and on the other, a plain wooden box: 'I Honour My Country'.

The Sultan summoned a great assembly of people
and arranged for the boxes to be placed on a table.
Then he called Fikirini and Hemedi and asked
them to choose a box each. When Fikirini chose the
box with 'I Seek Wealth And Fortune' inscribed
on it, and Hemedi chose 'I Honour My Country',
the Sultan knew at last that Hemedi was indeed his son,
for the son of a Sultan has no need to seek wealth
or fortune.

So the Sultan called Fikirini and Hemedi and gave
them each the boxes they had chosen. In Fikirini's
box there was a needle and thread, but in Hemedi's
box there was a crown.

Then the Sultan crowned Hemedi, and he reigned
as Sultan of Baghdad for many years. But Fikirini
was chased out of the land clutching his box and
never returned.

How Dog Learned To Use His Nose

Long ago, before Cat and Dog made friends with Man and found a place by his fire, they had to live in the wild and hunt for their own food. Dog depended on his sight and he was often hungry. For no sooner had he spotted a small animal to eat than it would disappear into the deep dark green forest, over stones, through tunnels and out of sight. But the clever Cat used his sense of smell as well as his sight, so he was able to catch up with all the small animals no matter where they ran, and he always came back from hunting with a full stomach.

One day Dog had had a very hard day. He'd chased Rabbit over and over again into the deep dark green forest, and each time Rabbit had escaped. The trouble was, Rabbit was the same colour as the brown earth in which he made his tunnels and Dog kept losing sight of him. He was so hungry and tired that he sat down in a clearing to rest. But it wasn't long before the deep dark green forest turned to black, and Dog realised that he would never be able to find his way home. He was beginning to get cold, and he was very frightened.

Just then, along came Cat. "What's wrong, Dog?" she asked him. "Why are you sitting there? Isn't it time you went home for the night?"

"I've been hunting all day, and I have caught nothing," said Dog, in a small tired voice. "Now that night has come I can't see my way home, and I am lost in this deep dark place."

"Don't worry," said Cat. "You can come and stay with me and share my food." And she led the way back to her house.

The next morning Dog went hunting with Cat in the deep dark green forest. He watched how easily Cat caught Rabbit and Mouse and Bird and he was surprised at her success. "Whenever I chase after Rabbit or any other animal, I lose sight of them," he said. "What makes you so clever?"

"It's easy," replied Cat. "I use my nose to sniff the smell of the animals wherever they go, so I can follow them even when I can't see them."

"Will you teach me how to use my nose?" asked Dog.

"All right," agreed Cat. "But you must listen carefully to me and do exactly what I tell you."

So Dog stayed with Cat and it wasn't long
before he, too, was able to use his nose to follow
the smells of smaller animals through the deep
dark green forest. With Cat's help he would chase
them over stones, through tunnels and into the
deepest darkest places and he never returned
hungry from hunting.

As time passed, Dog became fatter and fatter,
and more and more pleased with himself. "I can
manage quite well without Cat now," he thought.
And one day he woke up and wondered if he had
ever really needed Cat at all.

So he said to Cat, "I think I have learned all you can teach me now. I will go home to my family." But Cat replied, "Be patient, Dog. You may think you know everything but there is still more. Stay a few more days and you will know everything."

But Dog did not believe Cat and he became impatient. "She is just keeping me here because she needs me to help her hunt," he thought to himself. Then he said to Cat, "I used to think you were clever, but now I know just as much about hunting as you do. Why should I stay and listen to any more of your nonsense?"

Suddenly Cat ran off into the bush laughing. Dog was puzzled and decided to chase after her. He managed to follow Cat's smell and keep close behind her as she went over stones, through tunnels and into the deep dark green forest. When Dog at last reached the foot of a baobab tree, Cat's smell suddenly disappeared. Dog stopped and sniffed and then he ran round and round the tree, barking with excitement, until he became quite dizzy. Now and then he stopped, sniffed the air and then started to dash around it again. But no matter how many times he went round, he could not find Cat.

Cat, who was hiding high in the branches, found it hard to stay quiet while she watched Dog becoming more and more confused. Finally it was too much and she burst out laughing. Dog looked up in surprise. "Oh, there you are," he said, feeling very silly and a little annoyed.

49

"So you know as much about hunting as me, do you?" teased Cat. "Well, catch me now!" But Dog could not climb the tree and he crept away with his tail between his legs.

And that is why, even today, although Dog is very clever at following smells along the ground, he will never be quite as clever as Cat who can also chase her food up trees. Sometimes Dog pretends that he doesn't like Cat and doesn't care very much what she thinks. Secretly, though, he is still just a little embarrassed at the way Cat outwitted him that day in the deep dark green forest.

The Fisherman
And The Genie

(or 'One Good Turn Deserves Another')

Once upon a time there lived a very superstitious
fisherman. Whenever he went fishing he cast his
line only three times, and even if he hadn't caught
anything, he wouldn't fish again until the next day.

One day, when he cast his line for the first time, he caught a dead rat. "Yuk!" he said and threw it back. The second time he hooked an old rusty saucepan. "No use to anyone, and not a fish in sight!" he exclaimed, casting for the third and final time. This time he caught an old bottle. He was just about to chuck it back when it rubbed against the sleeve of his coat and he realised it was brass. "Well, at least I'll get a few pennies for this," he muttered to himself, as he began to shine it up.

Just then he heard a voice crying inside the bottle. "Good grief!" said the fisherman. "It sounds as if there's someone inside."

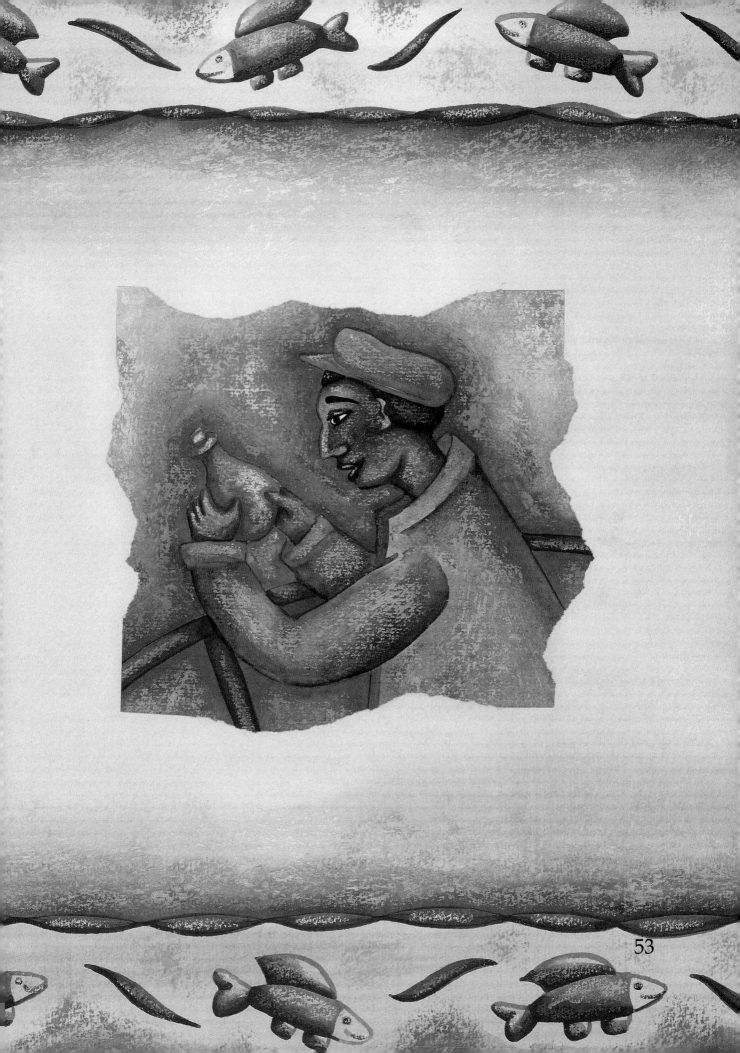

After struggling with the cork for a few minutes, he finally wrenched it off and out sprang a very tall Genie who laughed a loud wicked laugh, "Haaaaa! You are under my spell now and I'm going to make sure you have a really horrible time from now on!" he said.

"But why, oh Great One?" asked the fisherman. "Surely I've done you a favour by releasing you. And one good turn deserves another."

"I used to think that, too," replied the Genie. "But I changed my mind. I was shut up in this bottle by the prophet Suleman thousands of years ago and at first I swore an oath that if any man fished me up and let me out I would reward him with kindness. But over the years I got fed up with waiting, wasting my years away. I decided instead to do evil to the first person I saw." "That is so unfair, oh Great One," said the fisherman. "It is quite unreasonable of you, you know. And if you don't agree with me, let's ask the first three creatures we meet whether one good turn deserves another. If they agree with you, then I will accept my fate, but if they disagree, please won't you reconsider your decision?"

"All right," agreed the Genie reluctantly.

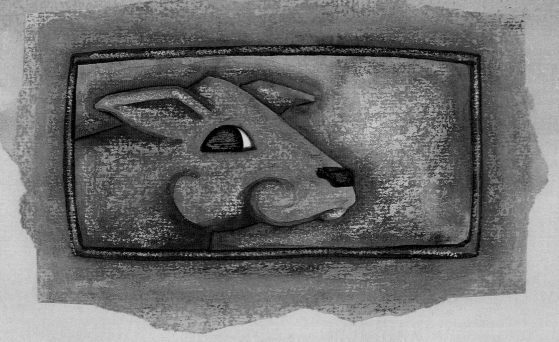

The first creature they met was a cow.
"Good morning, Mrs Cow," said the fisherman.

"Good morning, Fisherman," said Mrs Cow.

"Tell me, Mrs Cow," said the fisherman, "do you think one good turn deserves another?"

"Certainly not," replied Mrs Cow. "And I'll tell you why: we cows give people milk to drink - lots of it. You'd think they would be kind to us in return, wouldn't you? But when they've had enough they shoot us, eat us and make shoes from our skin." And the Genie said: "There you are Fisherman. You hear what she says?" And the fisherman knew that he had only two chances left.

So they walked on a little further until they reached a coconut tree. "Good morning, Mr Coconut Tree," said the fisherman.

"Good morning, Fisherman," said Mr Coconut Tree. "Tell me, Mr Coconut Tree," said the fisherman, "do you think one good turn deserves another?"

"Certainly not," replied the coconut tree. "And I'll tell you why: we coconut trees give people our coconuts and they cook the white flesh. When they are thirsty they drink the milk. We don't even complain when they take our skin to light fires with, and our husks to make rope with. We even make leaves for them to plait. You'd think they'd be kind to us in return, wouldn't you? But in the end they still cut us down and make us into door frames."

And the Genie said: "There you are Fisherman, you hear what he says?"

And the fisherman replied, "Yes, indeed, I hear it all but I still have one chance left, oh Great One."

So they walked on a little further and they met a wise old man.

And they asked him, "Do you think one good turn deserves another?"

"Why do you ask?" said the wise old man.

So they told him what Mrs Cow and Mr Coconut Tree had said. The wise old man thought for a moment; then he said, "I'm afraid I can't give you my opinion on this matter because I don't believe a word you have said."

"Why not?" asked the Genie and the fisherman together.

"Well," said the wise old man, "for a start how could a tall genie like you, oh Great One, possibly have squeezed into such a small bottle? I think you are trying to make a wise old man look foolish for believing you."

"You don't believe me, huh?" said the Genie.
"Well, watch this!" And he disappeared back into
the bottle. Then he shouted, "This is how I was."

The wise old man quickly popped the cork back into
the neck of the bottle. Then he said to the fisherman,
"My advice is to throw this bottle back, as far out
into the sea as you can, as quickly as possible."

So the fisherman carefully took the bottle to the
top of a high cliff and flung it as far as he could
into the sea.

So the next time you go to the seaside, think
carefully before you open any bottles which
have been washed onto the shore - you might
let the Genie out again!

Why Man No Longer Understands The Language Of The Animals

Long long ago there was a village in East Africa
called Arusha where people and animals spoke
the same language. In this village, the men and
women did not hunt the animals, but chose to live
on leaves and berries instead. The animals came
to trust the village people and shared with them
the secret of their language. The people built
shelters to keep the animals warm, and in return
the animals pulled carts to help the villagers
bring in the harvest. But the animals told the
villagers that if they ever shared the secret of
their language with other people they would be
made as deaf to it as was the rest of Africa.

Soon people from other villages heard about this
special relationship and they longed to know the
villagers' secret too. But the villagers would not
tell them because they were hunters and the
villagers knew they would only use their
knowledge to trap and kill the animals.

One day a rich young Sultan whose name was Kapere passed through that part of Africa. Hearing of the people and the animals of Arusha, he decided to visit the village. When he saw the animals and heard them talking to the villagers he was astonished. "Kumbe!*" he exclaimed. "How wonderful it would be if I too could understand what these animals were saying."

He stopped the first villager he saw and begged to know the secret. "I cannot tell you, Bwana*" said the man, whose name was Mwaliego. "I will give you all my money if only you will tell me," said Kapere. "Bwana, I cannot tell you or a terrible thing will happen. We will all become deaf to the animals," replied Mwaliego.

A little further along, Kapere stopped a second villager, and again begged to know the secret. "I cannot tell you, Bwana" said the man, whose name was Kyanda. "I will give you all my money and half my kingdom in return," said Kapere.

"Bwana, I cannot tell you or a terrible thing will happen. We will all become deaf to the animals," replied Kyanda.

Further along the road Kapere stopped a third villager, and again begged to know the secret.

"Bwana, I cannot tell you," replied the man, whose name was Daudi.

"I will give you all my money and all my kingdom in return," said Kapere.

Daudi hesitated. He was a very poor man and the offer did seem very tempting.

"Bwana, I still cannot tell you, or a terrible thing will happen. We will all become deaf to the animals," he said.

"Kumbe! Who told you that?" asked Kapere.

"The animals," replied Daudi.

"What nonsense!" said Kapere. "Don't you realise that they are just trying to trick you? How could they possibly make you deaf to their language when you know it so well?"

Daudi considered for a moment. He knew that Kapere's wealth and power would change his life forever. He would have everything he had ever dreamed of if he just shared his secret with one man. "What harm could it possibly do?" he thought to himself.

"All right," he agreed, and he did what he had been forbidden to do: he told him the secret.

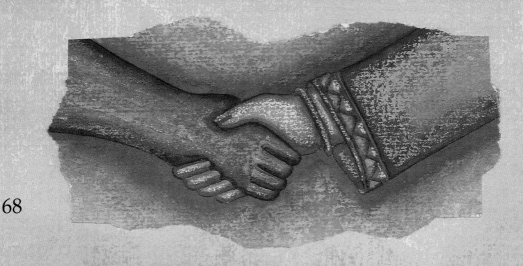

At once there was a terrible screaming sound as
the beautiful brown Hoopoe birds, with their regal
crests, who had been sitting in the dark green
mango trees above him, heard him betray them.
Soon they were joined by the noises of other birds:
Red Bishops, Hornbills, and Lourie birds. Then
came the noises of the other animals, as they heard
what the birds were saying and they joined in
with braying, mooing, neighing and oinking and
loud screeching. "What are those terrible sounds?"
the villagers asked each other as they looked
around them and up into the branches of the trees.
But the animals could no longer tell them. They
could only make the strangest of sounds.

Soon the villagers realised that one of them had betrayed the animals. They found Daudi and cast him out of the village but it was already too late. The animals had lost their trust in them and refused to speak to them ever again. And it wasn't long after that that the villagers started to hunt the animals with spears, just like their neighbours - and they still hunt them today.

* Kumbe! - "good gracious me!"
* Bwana - 'Sir' or 'Master'

72

The Man From The Next World

(or The Tale of the Two Foolish Women)

Long ago there lived a man, his wife, and their daughter. They were very poor and had only one cow for milk, and a small shamba* on which to grow their food. The man left early each morning to work in the fields, collecting food for the cow on his way home.

One night the daughter had a dream that she had grown up into a beautiful woman with a baby of her own. The next morning, after her father had left for work, her mother found her weeping and wailing inconsolably. "Whatever is the matter?" she asked. "I have lost my baby," cried the little girl. "I dreamed that I had a beautiful little girl but now that I have woken up she is no longer here." "That's terrible," said her mother and she too burst into loud weeping and wailing, so the air was filled with the terrible noise they were making.

Soon all the neighbours gathered round to find out what was the matter and when the foolish women told them, they roared with laughter. "How ridiculous!" they said. "We have never in all our lives heard such a fuss about a dream." But the mother and her daughter just continued to weep and wail loudly.

After a while the terrible noise began to annoy everyone. So the neighbours got together and thought up a clever plan to quieten the pair and have a party at the same time. "If you don't cheer your little girl up, she will die of grief," they said. "What shall I do?" wept the distraught mother. "You could throw a party - that would make her happy," said the neighbours. And they persuaded her to let them kill the cow and prepare a great feast for the village.

Later that evening the husband came back from work. When he heard what had happened he could hardly believe his ears. "In all my life I do not think I have ever met such a fool as you," he said to his wife. "How could you kill our only cow just because of a dream? I am leaving you. If I ever find anyone as foolish as you I will come back, but if not you will never see me again." And off he went, leaving his wife and daughter weeping and wailing more loudly than ever.

While he travelled the husband thought of ways to discover if there was anyone in the world more foolish than his wife. After a few days he came to a large town where he met a Wise Woman. He asked her, "Who is the most foolish person you know?" "The Sultan is a fool - but his wife is even more foolish - she believes anything anyone tells her," replied the Wise Woman. Then the man sat down to think of a plan to discover for himself whether the Sultana was indeed as foolish as his own wife.

The next morning the man wrote a letter which he carefully folded and put into an envelope before asking the Wise Woman for directions to the house of the Sultana.

When he arrived there he saw a pile of lime near the window of the house. And he dug down into the lime and covered himself in it so it flew about like smoke around his head, and then he shouted, "Help me! Help me, someone!"

The Sultana put her head out of the window and shouted down, "Who are you?" "I am a messenger from the next world," replied the man. "I have a letter to deliver to the Sultan's wife."

"Give it to me," ordered the Sultana, and she read the letter which went as follows:

"Greetings, oh beloved Niece. All is well in the next world and all your relations here are well but I am saddled with debt. I have borrowed some money but I have nothing left to repay my debtors. Please give a thousand gold coins to the messenger who gave you this letter so I can repay my debt. Greetings! signed, Your Uncle."

When the Sultan's wife read the letter, she was very sad and she went straight away to her room, unlocked her cash box, and took out a thousand gold coins. She also took out a cloak and some other small gifts for her uncle. Then she wrote a letter to him:

"Greetings, Uncle. Thank you for your letter. I am pleased you sent this messenger who brings news that you are in good health. I have given him the money and a few other items which I hope will be useful." And she gave the envelope and the bag of coins to the 'man from the next world' saying,

"Take all this to my uncle and tell him to let me know if he is still short of anything, and I will send more."

"Thank you," said the 'man from the next world' who hurried away, amazed that even among the nobility there were people as foolish as his own wife.

As the 'man from the next world' hurried home he passed some fields where he saw an old man hoeing his shamba. "I come from the next world to warn you of great danger," he said. "What danger?" replied the old man, startled. "The Sultan is on his way to kill you. He wants to offer you as a sacrifice to the gods so they will watch over his new house. But I have come to save you. Just wear my clothes and I will wear yours, so he won't recognise you," said the 'man from the next world'. The old man immediately did as he was told. Then the 'man from the next world' said, "Now, climb that coconut tree over there and keep an eye on the road to see if anyone is coming." The old man, who was so frightened he didn't suspect that he was being tricked, clambered up the tree as fast as his old limbs would allow.

Meanwhile the Sultan's wife had told her husband about the 'man from the next world' and had explained what she had done. The Sultan was furious. He shouted, "You foolish woman! Have you taken leave of your senses? Tell me at once which way this man has gone!" Then he saddled up his horse, put on his cloak, his turban and his curved broad-bladed dagger and galloped off after the thief.

The old gardener, who was clinging to the top of the coconut tree, could see the dust clouds rising as the Sultan galloped towards him, and he was terrified. "I can see him coming!" he shouted. But the 'man from the next world' just carried on hoeing. A few minutes later the Sultan arrived. He asked "Have you seen a man pass this way carrying a bag of money and an envelope?" The 'man from the next world' answered, "No, but there is a very strange man up that coconut tree over there. He came from the town and he says he is afraid of you. Perhaps he is the man you are looking for."

85

The Sultan was enraged and wanted to murder the man at the top of the coconut tree. He took off his cloak and his turban and his curved broad-bladed dagger so he had nothing on except a loincloth and he gave them to 'the man from the next world'. "Hold my horse," he ordered. Then he climbed the coconut tree, shouting to the poor old man at the top, "Now everyone will know what a wicked thief you are!"

The old man at the top of the tree realised that the 'man from the next world' had been right. The Sultan was indeed coming to kill him as a sacrifice for the gods! "What have I done to harm you? Please leave me alone, I am only a poor old gardener," he begged.

But the Sultan just continued to climb the coconut tree, and did not look down. Had he done so he would have seen the 'man from the next world' grasp his bag of money along with the envelope containing the Sultana's reply, don the Sultan's cloak, dagger and turban and gallop off on his horse as fast as he could.

"Where is that man going with your horse and your clothes?" the gardener asked the Sultan. Then the Sultan realised that he had been tricked and that he was just as foolish as his wife and he said to the old gardener, "Please come down and tell me your story."

And when the old man told the Sultan what had happened, and how frightened he had been by the news that he might be offered as a sacrifice to evil spirits the Sultan, instead of being angry, rocked with laughter. Then he told the old man how his wife, too, had been tricked by the 'man from the next world.' "We have all been such fools," they agreed, laughing until their sides ached.

Then the farmer asked the Sultan, "What will you tell your wife when you return home?" And the Sultan replied: "I don't want my wife to know that I am as foolish as she, so I shall tell her that I came upon the 'man from the next world' and that I was so touched by his story that I gave him my horse and all my clothing to take to those in the next world."

"That sounds like a good idea," laughed the old man.

The Sultan returned to his wife and did as he had told the old man, and the 'man from the next world' returned at last to his wife and daughter with his newfound wealth. "I am home!" he shouted, "and I have indeed found not one but three people as foolish as you." And so all was well again between them, but he did warn her, "If our daughter should ever have any more dreams which frighten her, please consult me before you do as the neighbours tell you!"

* Shamba - 'an allotment'

How The Snake Got His Eyes And The Millipede Got His Legs

Long, long ago the snake and the millipede lived in the same part of the forest and became the best of friends. In those days the slippery snake had eight hundred speedy legs but no bright eyes, so although he could run along the ground very fast indeed to catch his prey, he couldn't see it and had to rely on his sense of smell. He also lived in fear of larger animals who tried to creep up on him and make a meal of him.

Millipede, on the other hand, had two bright eyes, one on either side of his head, but he was not slippery and had no speedy legs. So although he could see what he wanted he could never get to it before it saw him and ran away.

For a long time the snake and the millipede lived together, and the millipede would watch out for signs of danger and other creatures to hunt, and then he would give directions to the snake who would either hide or run after the creature depending on which it was. It was a very satisfactory arrangement which suited them both well.

But one day Snake received a letter. He opened it and took it to Millipede who read it for him. "It's from King and Queen Lion," he said. "Read it, read it," said Snake impatiently.

"They are inviting you to the wedding of their son Prince Lion," said Millipede. "It's on Saturday at the Palace."

"Oh, how exciting!" exclaimed Snake. But then
he started to cry, a hissy sort of sound which
Millipede, who was his friend, could not bear
to hear.

"What's wrong?" he asked.

"Don't you know?" asked Snake, between
hissy sobs.

"No, it sounds like a wonderful invitation to me,"
said Millipede.

"But I won't be able to go. I can't see to find my way
and I'll be stamped on when the dancing begins
because I won't be able to see all those great big feet
coming towards me," sobbed the slippery Snake.

"Don't worry, my dear friend," said Millipede.
"If you will lend me your eight hundred speedy
legs for the evening, I will lend you my two bright
eyes. You will be able to see all the splendour and
join in with the festivities and I can run around
and get some exercise while you are gone."

And so it was agreed. Snake unbuckled each of his
eight hundred speedy legs and buckled them on
underneath Millipede. Then Millipede popped out
his two bright eyes and stuck one on each side of
Snake's head.

94

In almost the same moment as Millipede handed over his eyes and was plunged into darkness, Snake saw for the first time a whole new world. "It's amazing!" he said, as he looked up and saw the bright colours of the birds and animals in the beautiful forest. He had never imagined that the world was so colourful. There were mango trees and banana palms, through which the sun shone dappled on the forest floor. Then there were the oranges and bright greens of the Turaco parrots in the trees, the stripes of the beautiful zebras on the plains and hundreds of beautiful brightly coloured plants everywhere around him.

"Goodbye, dearest Millipede, you are so so kind," he hissed, as he slithered quickly away into the undergrowth, leaving poor Millipede hiding fearfully under a log because now, although he could run about with Snake's eight hundred speedy legs, he was completely blind.

Snake spent the most exciting evening of his life at the wedding. For the first time, he was able to see everyone and everything in brilliant splendour. He joined in with the dancing, he joined in with the singing, and he feasted until he was full. He was the happiest snake in the whole jungle.

When it was all over, and night had fallen, Snake set off back to where he had left Millipede. But when he was half way there, he paused and he looked this-a-way and he looked that-a-way and he saw what a blessing his newfound sight was. And he said to himself, "Why should I return these wonderful eyes to Millipede when I have everything I want now? For I can slither through the undergrowth, and hunt for myself and I can see my enemies and hide from them whenever I am being hunted. I will keep these wonderful eyes and pass them on to my children and my children's children."

So Millipede was left with Snake's eight hundred speedy legs, but he was blind and learned to stay hidden from danger, and Snake kept Millipede's two bright eyes and learned to hunt for himself. And to this day you will find Millipede hiding fearfully under stones and logs while Snake slithers stealthily through the grass hunting his prey.

But that's not the end of the story, for when the other creatures heard about what Snake had done he became feared and hated by all of them, and that is why today his only friends are other snakes.

The Clever Blacksmith

Once, long ago, there was a blacksmith who became famous for the quality of his excellent work. He made knives and spears for hunters, pick-axes for farmers and all kinds of other metal things - even jewellery for princesses.

Each morning he would pump the sheepskin bellows and make a roaring blaze to melt the metal, and he was so skilful that people near and far would flock to his forge just to have a chance to see the master blacksmith at work.

As he grew older, the blacksmith decided to take on an apprentice. Many young men applied for the job, but he chose Ali, a clever lad who was also hard-working, and for some years the old blacksmith spent his time teaching Ali all he knew.

As Ali's skill grew, he became the old blacksmith's pride and joy. "Look what Ali has done," he would say to people. "I couldn't have done it better myself." And as Ali became more and more confident in his work, the blacksmith entrusted him with more difficult tasks. Soon it was hard to tell his work apart from the old man's.

But Ali was changing too. No longer was he happy just to do as he was asked; he wanted to do things his own way. "I know better than you and I don't have to listen to you any more," he said to the old man one day. "Your work is very out of date. Perhaps it's time you retired!" The old man just smiled sadly, and said, "You are probably right, Ali, but remember that 'pride comes before a fall'."

It wasn't long afterwards that Ali decided to set up business on his own, but he still found time to drop in on the old blacksmith to crow about how much better he was doing and how much more money he was making.

"Are you still working with those old-fashioned tools?" he would ask, jingling the gold coins he had earned in his pocket. "Yes, they serve me well," replied the old man.

On one of these visits the old blacksmith asked Ali to help him work the bellows. "All right," agreed Ali reluctantly. "But I can't see why you don't go over to a machine. Bellows are old news these days."

As the old man worked away, Ali worked the bellows and sang a little song:

"Oh, who's the master blacksmith today?
It's me and you know what they say
I'm cleverer by far
I'm a risen star
And I'm earning twice your pay."

The blacksmith could see how arrogant Ali had become, but he stayed silent. Then he said to him, "Now come and help me beat this metal." Ali hesitated and looked at his watch. "I can't stay long," he said. "I need to get home to count my gold." But he grasped the hammer and beat on the anvil, while the blacksmith gently worked the bellows and whispered this song:

"Pride before a fall
Comes to one and all
You may be successful
But life can be stressful
Though you ride high, one day you may crawl."

Ali's reputation continued to spread like the sound of African drums beating, until it reached the ears of the Sultan who summoned him to his palace.

Ali lost no time in going round to see the old blacksmith to tell him his news: "The Sultan has sent for me! He must have heard of my reputation! I'm going to see him now and he'll make me the richest man in the kingdom."

Then he galloped off on his horse to the Sultan's palace, and stood before the great man himself.

"I have sent for you because I have heard that you are the most clever blacksmith in the land," said the Sultan.

"I am indeed," replied Ali.

"I have a very special task for you, and I do not want to be disappointed in your work," said the Sultan.

"No job's too big for me," said Ali confidently.

Then the Sultan called for his servants, who appeared with some iron rods.

"If you are as good as you say, this job will be all in a day's work for you," said the Sultan, handing over the iron rods. "Here is what I want you to do: make these rods into a real man by the end of the week. I don't mean a statue, but a thinking, walking, talking man. If you succeed I will make you the richest blacksmith in the land and you may marry my daughter. But if you fail, I shall have you put to death."

Ali was terrified. He went home and he sat with his head in his hands wondering how on earth he could make a real iron man. What could he do? He knew it was an impossible task, but he also knew that if he failed to carry out the Sultan's orders he would be put to death.

He asked all his friends and all his relatives but no one could tell him what to do.

At last he called at the house of his old master. He was working away at the anvil as usual, pumping the old sheepskin bellows and whistling softly to himself as he worked.

Ali bowed low before the old man and said, "Master, forgive me my pride and my arrogant ways. They are of no use to me now, for I will soon be dead."

"Whatever's the matter?" asked the old man. And when the young man explained his predicament he sat back in his chair and rocked with laughter. "You foolish boy," he said, but he said it in a kind, fatherly way. "Go to the Sultan and tell him that in order to carry out this task you need to use the charcoal of a banana tree."

Ali went back to the Sultan and told him what the old blacksmith had said. The Sultan immediately ordered a banana tree to be burned to the ground. But banana trees, as the old blacksmith knew, do not produce charcoal so the Sultan was forced to relent and Ali's life was saved.

When Ali returned to thank the master blacksmith he was full of humility and apologised again for his proud ways. "You warned me about my pride but I didn't listen to you. Now I know that it is you who is the master blacksmith because your age has brought you so much wisdom," he said.

From that day onwards the old blacksmith and his apprentice lived happily in the same town and stayed the best of friends.

Afterword

The origin of 'The Clever Rat' and most of the other animal stories in this book come from a book entitled *Hekaya za Abunuwas na Hadithi Nyingine* (Tales of Abunuwas and other Stories), first published in 1935 by Macmillan & Co.of London and regularly reprinted by Macmillans, Nairobi as a reader for schools in East Africa and now running beyond its forty-second imprint. These stories were probably handed down between generations who had no knowledge of writing and were thus part of the folklore of the Swahili people, their origin buried in the sands of antiquity.

'The Genie & the Bottle' in our tale is very similar to one of the stories in *The Arabian Nights*. The origin of those stories is not known either but the definitive edition of *The Arabian Nights* was first published as one volume in the United States in 1927 having originally been discovered in about 1727 by a French Orientalist when its title was '*The Thousand & One Nights*'. The flyleaf of the book reads:

"Two hundred years ago, Galland the famous French traveller and Orientalist, discovered *The Arabian Nights*. Since then they have been accepted as the most fascinating examples of the storyteller's art. Who, having read them, can ever forget these astounding stories of lion-hearted heroes and their madly loved ladies; of silken-clad beauties who turn from the murmuring of amorous verses to the devising of diabolical tortures for erring lovers! Where but in the East could love blossom so tenderly or distil so maddening a perfume! Only the passion and imagination of the Oriental could conjure up these stories of love and hate, poison and steel, treachery and black magic!"

In the introduction to our collection, Macmillans state that they are "Swahili stories told and written down by Africans put into standard orthography by a Reader of the Inter-territorial Language Committee of East Africa." This Committee consisted of a team of seventeen members convened by the three countries of East Africa (Kenya, Uganda and Tanganyika) in 1930. They standardised the spelling and grammar of the Swahili language in Roman letters, it previously having been only spoken, or written in Arabic. As far as we are aware, none of the stories has ever been published in English before.